WINNI ALLFOURS

Published in the United States by BridgeWater Books, an imprint of Troll Associates
First published in Great Britain 1993 by Hamish Hamilton Ltd

Printed in Italy.

10 9 8 7 6 5 4 3 2 1

WINNI ALLFOURS

Babette Cole

BridgeWater Books

Winni Allfours wanted a pony more than anything else in the world.

There were ponies by the bus stop.

Winni always missed
the school bus.

"Please," pleaded Winni.
"No!" said her mom and dad,
who were very strict and
only ate vegetables.
"We don't approve
of people who
own ponies."

"But I only want a little one!" said Winni.

"I don't want to hear any more about it," said her mom. "Sit down and eat your vegetables."

"And no more of those nasty hamburgers and French fries for lunch at school!" said her dad.

"You'll turn into a horse if you keep eating so many carrots," said the lady in the school cafeteria.

"What a brilliant
idea!" said Winni.

So Winni ate and ate.
She ate up all her vegetables.
"Good girl!" said her mom and dad.

Very slowly

to

things   started

happen....

Her parents were horrified.
"She's eating my lawn and flower beds!"
said her dad.

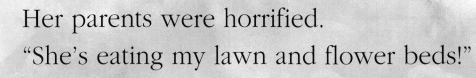

"What are we going to do?" shrieked her mom.
"She's ruined the organic vegetable patch!"
"Serves them right!"
said Winni.

But Winni knew just what to do.

She jumped the wall and joined the bus-stop ponies!

She loved racing around with them.

"Hey, Winni," said her new friend, Snowdrop,
"you're real fast. You should
meet my owner, Paddy.
He's a racehorse
trainer!"

"Good heavens," said Paddy, when he saw
Winni run. "She's a Triple Crown winner!"

So he took Winni off to Kentucky to start training to be a racehorse.

Bye!

See You Soon Winni   Good Luck!

PADDY REGAN
INTERNATIONAL RACE HORSES

"This is much better than school!" said Winni.

"You should be very proud of your daughter," said Paddy. But her parents were still horrified.

Mr. and Mrs. Allfours were not, however, the only people watching Winni run.

Nobbler O'Toole, the horse dealer, wanted to buy
Winni so that he could sell her for lots of money.
"Certainly not!" said her mom. "We couldn't
possibly sell our daughter!"

So the night before the big race,
Nobbler sent his men to steal Winni.

But when they
stopped at an inn,
Winni stole the truck!
"That's no ordinary
horse!" they said.

She drove straight to the racetrack.
Luckily, her parents had come to watch.

"Come on, Dad!" said Winni. "I need your help!"

"Hang on, Dad!" said Winni, as they flew past the finish line.

Dad was scared stiff!
But they beat the world record.

Winni won lots of money for everyone.
But her dad had a
very sore bottom!

"If we gave you lots of hamburgers and French fries to eat," said her mom, "you would change back into a little girl. Then we'd buy you a pony."

"But if I were a girl, I'd have to go back to school!" said Winni. "No thanks. This is far more fun!"